Chasing the Zombie

Erick Hoffman

Supremium Publishing

Copyright © 2013 by Erick Hoffman.
Published by Supremium Publishing

The characters and events portrayed in this book are fictitious. Any similarity to real persons, living or dead, is coincidental and not intended by the author.

Summary: A zombie tries to break from his flesh problems by telling his own unique personal stories, and those of his very interesting hoard.

ISBN: 978-0-9910583-2-7 (hardback) / 978-0-9910583-1-0 (paperback)

Visit: http://mysite.verizon.net/vze194pkt/

Dedicated to my everything, my wife.

I LOVE YOU!

Acknowledgements

A special thank you to my wife Melissa, Theresa, Dave, Bob, and Brian who listened and helped clean up the ramblings of a zombie fanatic. A special acknowledgement to zombies, stop scaring the crap out of me!

Contents

Preface

The drudgery of the unusual routine stirred. Cravings were always first. Why must they consistently overtake my incarnate desires? Sprinkle in a fair amount of chewing, biting and finally the swallowing. I always want to skip straight to the overly gratifying wonderful swallowing.

This has been tried, but alas it never provided the same level of pure ecstasy obtained by the entire process. Maybe, yeah I think I will try it again.

Chasing the zombie described how the rather large, unlikely hoard I have decided to partner with jokingly labeled the unusual routine. My life can be summed up by a very unoriginal twist to terminology reserved for heroin addicts! I swear I have heard this description before. Anyway, I must come to terms with or maybe find a way to overcome my haunting routine.

Should I turn to a life once lived? Would this champion a way out of this routine? Unearthed personal reflections from my hoard should provide for some entertainment or at least something to fill a zombie life less ordinary.

Random thoughts of my human life's personal revelations accompanied with my new acquaintances overwhelm me. I embarked on a new, surely perilous journey serving as a zombie scribe. The stories told remind me that I haven't been alive in what feels like forever.

Feverishly the cravings are fought back clouding every reflection, thought, and memory. Finally, the strength is summoned to formulate a complete and let's just call it a hopefully coherent regurgitation. A career forever bonded to a myth was the beginning.

Chapter 1
An Assignment

Honey and Beeswax made the well-aged CEO very wealthy. He spoke with a strong thick German accent. To comprehend him one needed to focus intently on his spoken words. Many said it sounded like he spoke with a mouth full of marbles.

A thick blond head of hair sat upon his literally and figuratively big head. The hair was overly conditioned, and groomed to the point of perfection. His hair helped him with a personal initiative to try to fit in. However, he looked more like a wannabe, as he put his hair in a ponytail for the company's casual Friday's. Employees automatically saw through this gimmick. They knew this was a futile effort to try to fit in. He definitely was not pretty "fly" for a white guy!

Standing over six feet tall and stocky, his presence easily overtook any board room. He ruled his kingdom, I mean his company, with absolute authority, much like a

Viking Warrior. All knew their place as no one dared solicit a challenge. Those who dared were quickly and violently shown the unfiltered rage of the CEO.

His demeanor and physical characteristics forever likened him to be of Viking descent. Never verified, more water cooler talk than anything else. It was further exacerbated during the company's annual gathering.

Held at the end of the year, the event was well over the top. Champagne flowed like waterfalls and food was personally served, which catered to the most selfish of appetites. It was no surprise that the event resembled the ocean, as Lobsters, Black King Kong Shrimp, Pacific Blue Fin Tuna, and Beluga Caviar flooded the room.

The company used this event to strategize for the next business year. Heavy on everyone's mind was the well invested in, soon to be released commercially, wonder drug. The drug was deemed by the company to be the cure-all of all cure-alls. A gorgeous crystal case displayed the syringe containing the revered drug of the future, which was to be unveiled at this function.

A single assignment, which varied year to year, accompanied the event. This time employees were to create a unique, original story. The subject was directed towards what the company commonly joked was the hardest and most dedicated worker; the bee. Also, for the first time the CEO was to participate.

There was only one single caveat for the assignment which involved the stories presentation. Stories were to be presented through a simple podium reading. No props allowed, just the person and his or her voice.

The cash award for the most creative story was $50,000. Upping the ante, the CEO included his personal Hawaii timeshare, considered the holy grail of timeshares. The retail value was estimated to be well over the cash award. The timeshare was a frequent incentive used by the company, usually reserved for the company's top performer. No, the "bee" never received the award.

The CEO definitely upped the level of competition by his participation. As this was his assignment, the CEO would use his own words to weave an ancient, little known Viking myth.

Chapter 2
Myth

This was the King of all Kings or so the King thought. Narcissism is probably one of his better characteristics. The haughty visions of his absolute grandeur would plague his destiny and kingdom.

The tyrannical King waged war on all who defied him. Merciless and unforgiving blood-spattered battles rained across the land. His army without question always blissfully obliged. Until the gods gave him what he believed to be his true birthright, to become a god, the battles would only increase in size and violence.

The King's body was cocked back, beet red, and shaking. His routine of heavenly shouts were about to begin. Screams aimed towards the heavens, so thunderous they could rouse the dead.

"Now!"

"You dare defy my right!"

"Worship me and sing my praises!"

"You bestow upon me my right!"

"Now!"

The old exulted King was to blame for his son's over-exaggerated sense of self-worth, although he quietly expressed similar feelings. Desired yes, however never demanded like his son. He prayed his grandchildren would not repeat this rhetoric.

Weary of this arrogance, the gods determined that it was time to chastise the King. A punishment void of any mercy would be unleashed. Unfortunately for the King, the gods were so irked that Loki the god of Pranks was tasked.

Loki had a demonically evil quick wit, easily the most callous of all gods. Humanity feared his ingenious cruelty and total lack of sympathy. The duck billed platypus beautifully illustrated his complete sense of heartlessness.

A duck happily waddled along when it unfortunately crossed paths with Loki. A beaver and an otter were off in the distance busily constructing their homes in a nearby river. Bored, searching for a first-rate laugh, he swoops up all three. Effortlessly and methodically the animals were toyed with. A variety of body parts were wickedly mixed and matched with calculated, vindictive twists and turns, much like a Rubik's Cube.

The toyed animals failed to provide him with the entertainment impossibly expected. He tossed the three animals in his mouth. Quickly pulverized, the helpless animals are soon spit out. A jumbled mess of a creature has been created.

The duck billed platypus slowly opened its eyes, focused on what it believed to be his new parent. A cruel twisted smile is displayed as Loki simply saunters off.

Gladly taking on the assignment a most dastardly plan was concocted. The gods only gave one stipulation. The King would be required to indefinitely relive the punishment. This must be remembered throughout the rest of humanity's existence.

The plan involved what all the gods had developed a disdain for centuries ago; bees. A swarm of bees had stung and killed their favorite of all animals, the unicorn. The gods so enraged, slowly inflated the swarm, which caused them to burst. Only a single overly inflated bee remained. The lone bee's dimensions resembled a nice round melon. Helplessly, tirelessly the bee flapped itself into complete and utter exhaustion.

Loki laughed at this pitiful sight and proceeded to kick the bee over and over again. Eventually the bee exploded, which ended his fun. For Loki the bee fun had just begun.

Loki obtained five bees with the intent of creating a swinging hanging bee thing. The wings from five bees were removed. Next these bees were inflated to the size of an orange. Finally, by their stingers, the bees were stuck into a level tree branch. The bees now dangled helplessly, of equal distance, side by side. Loki took the bee on the left hand side and flung it at the bee located next to it, which created a constant swinging motion. This would later become known as Newton's Cradle or as most refer to it as the swinging hanging ball thing.

Loki often watched his contraption to formulate his wickedly evil plans. He had finally come up with the Kings punishment. This of course involved bees.

He summoned and then sucked into his mouth a swarm of bees. While inside him the bee's venom was infected. The bees were then released with a thunderous blow, sent in the direction of the King's villagers.

A high volume of loud moans were heard. Watch standers hurriedly surveyed the area, baffled as to see their own villagers awkwardly heading towards them. A lone scout was summoned and sent off to ascertain the situation.

A deafening, brief scream was heard. No scout returned. Next, a scouting party was sent out with an armament of men.

Again, ear-piercing screams. Some return.

At first glance the survivors were smeared with blood and appeared to have bite marks. As they drew closer limbs were absent and chunks of flesh barely hung on. They spoke of crazed villagers who moaned, stumbled and chomped on anyone within reach. Now these same villagers amassed themselves before the army.

The King's army had met its match. Most soldiers were unable to even muster the slightest defense. How could they? These were their mothers, wives and children. The villagers however, did not share these feelings or hesitations. They easily made their way through the army. Now the King was in their sights.

Loki watched with heavenly delight as the hoard closed in on the King. The King's fight was brief at best. Silence soon replaced his sword, as he was overwhelmed and covered in villagers and soldiers alike.

Before the King was completely devoured by his countrymen, the swarm of bees and "humans" were summoned back by Loki. The venom was now rendered useless. This caused the villagers to experience sharp pains near the lower right area of their abdomen.

Loki would now punish the King. A punishment of an undead ghoul that hungered for human flesh, which would forever, wander the earth. Grudgingly the King took his new throne, as the King of all zombies.

Chapter 3
Table 6

Pure adulation roared from the standing room only audience. Over-the-top cattle calls and booming cheers easily made the CEO's presentation the day's best. Although the obvious winner CEO graciously deferred, the group from Table 6 would be this year's winner.

Their submittal was nothing to note, it also reeked of minimal effort. A dreadful story was made up that centered on a horrifying creature know as the "beezard," half bee and half buzzard. It won more for the play on words, than for the story itself.

Around table 6 seated a group of coworkers who were at one time exceptionally close. The dynamic shifted to slightly uncomfortable when two from the group began a relationship. Jill and Max would go from casual friends, to lovers, and then into marriage.

What better time to rekindle their friendship than over a nice cash prize and a free Hawaiian vacation. Most importantly they celebrated the open bar. Their poison was several rounds of Zombies, a cocktail made of fruit juices, liqueurs, and a variety of rums.

Max had been on a very light diet, unable to take part in the groups over indulgences. His eating and drinking habits changed due to chronic stomach pains. The group was not taking it easy on Max laying a slew of "you light weight" and "drink up buttercup" comments throughout the evening.

Max's retort was silence until his slow dim wit drummed up a dreadful comeback. If not for the drunkards at the table it would have fallen very flat. He joked that he was the table's designated driver, as the group had driven him bonkers.

Suddenly, Max grabbed his stomach as he barreled over in agonizing pain. Jill immediately leaped into action, as her father had passed from similar symptoms. Max's appendix had burst.

Jill hurdled a waitress and made a bee line for the display case. She reached it, only to find it difficult to open.

Frustrated, she lifted it over her head and slammed it to the ground. The wonder drug was free of its container.

Hastily she returned and injected Max with the wonder drug. After several minutes he was miraculously and completely healed. He now found himself hungry. Not a little, but a lot. Relieved, the group celebrated Max's new found health.

Quickly several drinks were ordered and downed by Max. He transitioned from dud to stud and became the life of the party. Unable to control his mouth, he released the news of the couple's pregnancy. Max was too drunk to care that Jill was steamed, as they had planned to tell their families first.

Chapter 4
Bakers' New

Jill and Max Baker were that couple who had their entire lives mapped out. Kids were mentioned, but their careers came first. After a few years, the idea of having children came up again. Unsuccessful in their efforts, they both went through fertility testing. It was revealed that Max's sperm were slow, or as they joked, he "had the slowest swimmers in the pond." Baby plans were again put on hiatus. As an extra precaution Jill went on birth control, which would provide the protection of any unexpected oopsies.

How could Jill be pregnant? Jill suspected, but she couldn't be pregnant. Could she? A pregnancy test was soon purchased. She eventually found herself in the bathroom staring at the blue plus sign. Completely taken aback, she bought another pregnancy test. Same result. Jill told Max.

Max was astonished and wanted to make absolutely sure. The accuracy of the test would need to be confirmed.

He purchased his own kit and now it was his turn. No blue sign for Max, clearly he was not pregnant. The happy couple embraced, especially after they later found out that they were expecting not one, not two, but three little blessings. As soon as the parents could, they found out the sex of the babies.

Chapter 5
Medicine Cabinet

Not everyone celebrated the wonder drug and the Bakers' news. Table 6 had made a terrible mess. When Max lurched over in pain, all the table's contents had been knocked over onto the floor. The bulldozed waitress added to the mayhem. The waitress tried to regain her balance on the two carts she had busily pushed. A loud crash was heard and as she brought both carts down. A majority of the day's dirty dishes lay broken and shattered on the floor.

The chaos caused by Table 6 shifted the entire staff's night from bad to worse. The event was stressful enough for the scant crew. Johnny, already overworked, would be forced to do even more. He was busily scrubbing pots when he was called from the kitchen to help clean up the mess.

Johnny grumbled and then commented, "Wow! This was a rough one."

"Two double shifts are two too many."

"Now I will have to stay late, again."

"This just sucks!"

Johnny hated this job, especially as he had reached a slight level of notoriety as a professional wrestler. He often felt degraded, as he was forced to supplement his income with what he deemed a menial job. Hopefully his next match would move him into the limelight. It would be difficult, since he now found himself completely exhausted. How could he even make or perform well at his next match? Thankfully, his medicine cabinet should provide the answer.

The lighting in his bathroom was weak. He glared at his reflection in the crookedly hung medicine cabinet. Clicking was heard as the cabinet was slowly pushed in and opened. The poorly placed, small cabinet made all of its contents touch each other.

It was not what he needed. He wanted to get high. His choices were limited to the two bottles in front of him. A small bottle of white pills and a large bottle of children's vitamins.

The white pill bottle's label was so old and degraded that it was illegible. He couldn't remember what the contents were, as he had purchased them some time ago. They may have been for allergies or relief of chronic severe gas pains.

He had played with the white pills before and wound up in a ditch in a not very nice neighborhood. The worst part was not where he wound up, but that he was left with an inability to (alleviate via number two) for weeks. It was the children's vitamins turn. He had not purchased them. The vitamins were probably left by a prior tenant. Any sort of high will do, so he decided to roll the dice. Before attempting to open the bottle he thought, "What was the world coming to? Children zombie vitamins, really?"

The childproof lid presented some challenge. Under his breath he mumbled, "Stupid lid." He had developed a severe contempt for these lids. While he struggled with the bottle, he experienced a flashback to his childhood.

Chapter 6
Remote Memory

Why are the most painful memories always at the forefront of our minds? Why can't they be shaken? A fractured, wasted youth clouded his memory. Maybe it would be better just to skip the match and not dredge up his childhood "glory" days.

The only thing his childhood helped him develop was a defense mechanism of stinging sarcasm. Walls were built around this sarcasm, which allowed no one to truly get to know him. His father would often beat him for his sarcastic remarks. This was to remind him that sarcasm was the lowest form of wit.

He was a goofy and nerdy kid, who had grown up in an abysmally tough neighborhood. Diagnosed with Perthes, a rare hip disorder, forced him to wear a leg brace for most of his childhood. It was bad enough he had to go to school with this brace on, but there was no way he would venture out to the playground jungle. Playgrounds were ruled by bullies. These same kids would rather kick your teeth in than have a sleepover. This led to a childhood bound in front of the television.

What was on the boob tube? The answer was always the same. Over a hundred channels with nothing but the same crap. The remote control only made the crap appear that much faster.

One day the remote control stopped working. After the remote broke, his parents would joke that Johnny was the much more expensive remote replacement. Funny at first, it was annoying when repeated indefinitely. His father took it one step further when he stated that this was a job worthy of Johnny's talents, given that he always pushed his father's buttons.

Johnny's channel surfing was usually futile. He really just wanted to find his favorite show, The Zombie Awesome Posse. You may remember the theme song:

"They may or may not have your back cause you could be their snack, The Zombie Awesome Posse. They'll take your brain if that's the only way, The Zombie Awesome Posse."

Some honey company sponsored the show. The only reason he remembered was the company's constant interruption of commercials. The show was a ratings bonanza.

Popular with all ages, the cartoon smash was usually on an endless 24 hour cycle. The Zombie Awesome Posse referred to themselves as ZAPies. They fought the most extremely unbelievable evils of humanity and zombie kind.

The shows brain breaks were his personal favorite. At any point during the show the ZAPies would be forced to hook up to the brain wave inerter, which resembled the chair where someone's grandma would get her perm done.

Much like grandma's perm chair, a big dome would be placed over the ZAPies head. The inerter sent an electronic impulse to the ZAPies brains, effectively feeding the zombies' brain requirement. Thankfully, the posse had never actually eaten any brains, or so the show's creator wanted you to think.

The original characters featured: Ultra Z (Leader of the ZAPies. Ultra Z had super zombie strength, equivalent to 100 zombies.); Princess Z's (Heir to the Zombie throne with an ability to induce a sleeplike state. Rumored to be romantically linked to Ultra Z.); Brains Pain (Near genius level for a zombie and able to control both zombie and human thought.); Switchy (Morphing powers, which can merge a zombie and human into a single being.); and the Fashion Triplets (Incredible and fabulous fashion sense, their powers increase based on the enemies fashion faux pas.).

Episode 1 - The one hour world premiere.

The deepest darkest bowels of the unknown could no longer hold this monster back. The enormous, hideous monstrosity was now released upon us. Who could save us? Better yet, can any one save us? All who have tried only ended in epic failure. Half the town had been devoured.

Could it be? Yes! It's, The Zombie Awesome Posse. They'll surely send this monster back to where it came from.

Ultra Z attacked first. Caring not for his own safety, he headed straight on to tackle the monster. His head struck the stomach of the monster like a comet violently striking the earth. Loud booming noises were heard, but they were not from the monster. Nay, the noises poured out of a multiple number of melodious orifices. All were equally horrendous. A disgustingly loud BUUUURRRRhuuumm was launched from the monsters mouth. This burp, more of a "Vurp", lands as a direct hit on Ultra Z. No one knew if it was the force or smell that crumbled Ultra Z. Ultra Z was hurt and hurt bad.

Princess Z was now on the scene. The monster's thick pulsating skull was way too hard for her powers of siesta to penetrate. Finally she did it! The monster was now catching some Z's. Catnapping was a more suitable term. Much like a father who woke up suddenly from a deep slumber, the monster was grumpy. If they thought the monster was mad before, it now appeared much more enraged.

Brain Pain used his mental powers. The happiest thought has been placed in the monsters mind. The mental image was of destruction and gobbling up the helpless victims. A most evil of smirk appeared on the monster's face. Could this become a permanent state of eternal bliss? Sadly, the monster suffered from a mild form of attention deficit disorder and was easily distracted as a butterfly passed by. The butterfly quickly flew out of the monster's sight. The rampage continued.

Creating a monster of their own was Switchy's idea, hurriedly morphing whatever humans and zombies were around. Brain Pain quickly took control of the ZAPies' creation. The two monsters engaged in battle. Things definitely looked up as the ZAPies' monster pummeled the other monster.

"Yikes!" The battle was over before it even began as the ZAPies were forced to take their mandatory brain break.

This doomed their monster, as it was left without conscious thought. It stood, a mindless sack of nothing, to be inevitably devoured. The recharged ZAPies returned to find a bloody puddle where their monster once stood.

The Fashion Triplets took center stage with a brilliant idea. Unfortunately even the Fashion Triplets powers were limited. They quickly used their powers to make a pair of really, really high, clear colored heels. There was no color combination that could possibly match the monsters atrocious outfit.

The ZAPies placed the heels near the "cliffs of no bottom." Brain Pain was able to temporarily take control of the monsters mind. Never having worn heels before, the monster was unable to stand and fell clumsily towards the "cliffs of no bottom." The monster barely avoided falling off the cliff and re-engaged the ZAPies. Ultra Z had a new plan and quickly found the largest mirror made. As the monster was barreling down, Ultra Z zoomed in with the mirror. The monster caught its reflection and ran away in complete and utter embarrassment, never to be seen again.

"Go Zombie Awesome Posse! Yeah!"

Kids wanted to be the show's zombie characters. The characters easily took over the top spot as the number one selling Halloween costume. Johnny dressed up for several Halloweens as Ultra Z. He fancied himself as both a super-hero and professional wrestler. Johnny had now finished his trip down memory lane and continued his unscheduled wrestling match with his children's vitamins.

Chapter 7
Re-energized

Success!

Finally the bottle was opened. Johnny dug out the two lone vitamins. The selected pills were shaped like a bulky, muscular, well groomed zombie. They now lay atop the bathroom counter.

Stupid lid, again!

He only had a minimal battle to secure the bottle.

Now as to the selection of his high, immediate or slow.

Sorted, crushed, baked, pick a toe...

Sorted, crushed, snort....

Where is that darn foil?

Johnny mumbled to himself, "I'm not going to snort." Snorting caused his nose to swell up. People would be able to tell that Johnny did drugs. If he picked injecting, it must go between his toes. While not the fastest way of getting the desired results, it would at least hide his addiction.

Where is that darn foil?

Hello, there it is.

Two vitamins were crushed into a powder-like form and gently placed in the center of the foil. He pulled out a Zippo, snapped his fingers and ignited the flint. The sound of snapping and popping was heard as the vitamins baked. A needle quickly consumed the liquefied vitamins.

He pondered to himself, "Eeny, meeny, miny, moe, the needle goes between these toes." His eyes rolled back in his head. A decent size rush came upon him.

He sprung to his feet shouting, "Oh yeah! It's go time!"

Chapter 8
The Match

A children's vitamin eventually consumed the entire sports world. Olympians and professional athletes alike found themselves inventing ways to abuse these pills. The abuse became so rampant that a special test was created to detect abusers.

The term *chasing the zombie* was coined, as the vitamin featured zombie-like characters. To chase, one needed to melt down and immediately inject the vitamin into the blood stream. A professional wrestler discovered a longer more profound effect when the drug was combined with the consumption of human flesh.

The wrestler's discovery came during the undercard of the wrestling match of the millennium. While not the top billing, he was still a fan favorite. The match slated Johnny Flash-in-D-Pants vs. Two-Times-Your-Zip-Code Jones, better known as Zip Code. Zip Code easily weighed more than 500 pounds.

The overly scripted match was going according to plan until Johnny accidently bit Jones when a clothes line caught Johnny directly in the mouth. Johnny began to stumble, moan, and then exhibited signs of superhuman strength. Johnny proceeded to get up and then threw Jones from one side of the ring to the other. The crowd erupted in applause and charged the stage. A booming roar was heard, "PANTS!" "PANTS!" "PANTS!" Johnny definitely loved every minute of that.

The toast of the town, Johnny woke up the next morning feeling drunk with joy. He had several missed messages from his fellow wrestlers. The president of the wrestling company even called, he wanted to congratulate Johnny and setup a shot at the title. This would come with several scheduled meet-and-greets with fans.

Johnny was on cloud nine. However he experienced a strange, new craving. It was one he had never had before. He couldn't even put a finger on it. It did not control him, it merely annoyed him. He easily shook the cravings away as the high from the previous day still encompassed him. The cravings, however, would return.

He entered the late night 24-hour pharmacy and quickly proceeded to the vitamin aisle. Finally, some luck! This was the first store in a while that carried his precious vitamins. He snatched all bottles, as his cravings were getting worse.

Fumbling through his wallet, he found his credit card. Shaking, he gave his card to the cashier. The cashier stared, and asked if he was alright. Johnny stated he was fine, finalized the purchase, and snatched the bag. He left for home to repeat his new ritual to quiet the cravings and prepare for the next day's match.

The title match was underway, Johnny battled against POOR LITTLE RICH LOU. The script called for a similar clothesline with the inevitable bite. It was not to be a simple bite, but a chunk of flesh. A fake piece of flesh was pasted on and would be ripped off then ingested.

Lou went for the clothesline, but it was with the wrong arm. Lou assumes Johnny will adjust and the bite would be performed later. Of course, the crowd knew nothing of this, only the wrestlers did.

Lou's screams, temporarily silenced the crowd. Unfortunately for Lou, Johnny had not adjusted. A large chunk of flesh was suddenly missing. Overdramatically, Johnny chewed then swallowed the flesh.

Unlike his temporarily burst of strength in the previous match, he had an extended show of even greater strength. Johnny performed several over-the-head presses with a sopping and bloody Lou. The crowd erupted, counting each press, 1, 2, 3…

Johnny won the match and was now the undisputed champion. A meet-and-greet was scheduled to showcase the new champion. Johnny did not look forward to the fan meet-and-greet. He loved his fans, but dreaded sitting around for endless hours chit chatting.

During the $25 per person fan meet-and-greet, Chad a super fan, talked Johnny's ear off. Chad asked questions primarily about Johnny's superhuman strength. About to learn Johnny's secret, Chad's phone began to ring. A text appeared on his phone.

"Where are you?"

Two seconds later.

"You need to call me!"

Chad quickly silenced his phone.

Johnny just wanted to shut Chad up and was about to reveal his secret to get rid of this kid. The momentary distraction allowed Johnny to rethink. It would now cost Chad $100 for the secret. Bitterly Chad shelled out the money, and then left the event fuming. Now was the time to deal with his nagging problem.

Chapter 9
Bad Break

The subject of the text read:

"IT IS YOU, NOT ME! WE ARE DONE!"

Jessica could not believe it. Her boyfriend was breaking up with her by a text. The initial shock of the text did not last long. There would be hell to pay and a heated text showed her anger.

"Who breaks up with someone over a text? I'll tell you who, A COWARD! You are a spineless JERK!"

It had been some time since their split and Jessica had put on an extra 20 pounds. She had already put on an extra 15 pounds during her freshman year of college. This was the real reason Chad choose to split with Jessica, not her annoying personality.

Chad was very self-absorbed. His muscle shirts and tank tops were the only outfits he could be seen in. He really preferred to be shirtless. This was brought to new levels as he prepared for a potential career in professional wrestling. There was little room in his outfits for his absolutely huge self-indulging attitude.

Jessica was no saint either. She had developed her mother's domineering attitude and had a general lack of empathy for the opposite sex. Her mother was a loud-mouth. Her booming voice would resonate throughout the neighborhood at all times of the day. It was directed primarily at her poor husband.

Her husband never seemed to want to hear the tirade. He never did anything about it, unless you consider avoidance a solution. When he got home from work he would slowly pull into the driveway. Ten to twenty minutes later he would slump out of his car. Sometimes he entered the house, often not. It didn't matter much though, his wife could just as easily yell at him while he was in the car, and frequently did.

Jessica pretty much treated Chad like her mother treated her father. After the breakup, Jessica would constantly call, email and follow Chad. This was the reason Chad slapped her with a restraining order. This mere piece of paper was no challenge for the loudmouthed Jessica.

She purchased the most expensive electronic measuring device currently on the market to ensure the 50-foot rule was obeyed. Chad could see her vigor and utter disdain while she beamed the device at him. Then indirectly, she would verbally attack Chad. Often saying that no man was going to disrespect her and how she wished all her past boyfriends were dead.

Unable to deal with the breakup, Jessica eventually sank into a deep depression. Jessica went to a psychiatrist who labeled her with clinical depression and placed her on a new all natural anti-depression drug.

The staticky intercom blasted, "Jessica Sanders, your prescription is ready."

Finally, she thought to herself. It had almost taken 20 minutes to fill her prescription. Bounding up to the counter, she tapped her fingernails until the pharmacist "finally" acknowledged her. She snatched the package and headed out to her car. She sat in her car and read the ingredients, as she thought it funny that an anti-depressant drug could be all natural.

"Honey Number 5 and Other Dark Honeys, Water, Natural Flavors, Vitamin C, and Natural Fruit Acid."

She thought this really was all natural. Suddenly she began to cry and recalled the first time she and Chad met.

Chapter 10
Early Licking

Rated number 5 out of 100 of the best US Pre-K's made this school one of the most prestigious. Legacies were those of billionaires, past presidents, and famous actors. Only the well-connected got into this school.

The overly intrusive, extensive and expensive entrance application was more for show. Future attendees were typically known even before the application was reviewed. Applicants knew this, but still shelled out the $2,000 application process fee in hopes their child would get in. The fee was paid up front and was non-refundable.

Parents had to list their child's short comings. It was well known that this was a "make it or break it" question. Specifically stating:

No child is perfect, nor should they be. You are required to identify at a minimum three of your child's unique short comings. Do not state that your child is too perfect or that your child has no faults. Failure to follow these specific instructions will lead to an automatic rejection of your application. (Reminder: Your deposit is non-refundable.)

Jessica's parents did list her unique short comings:

1. Jessica speaks with a small lisp, specifically having issues with the letter R.
2. Jessica is a tender soul. She is sensitive and needs constant praise.
3. Jessica has recently developed a propensity for licking. She has recently started licking. This can best be likened to a dog licking a person. Our family pet dog, Jenkers, loves to lick and adores little Jessica. We believe this is where she learned this aberrant behavior.

The school appreciated the real answer, as Jessica's propensity for licking was honest and unique. It was never communicated, but this is how Jessica made it into the school. However, the school would eventually regret their decision.

Weather forecasters mentioned nothing of rain, however little Chad was soaked. It was not rainwater, but saliva. Everyone knew Jessica was the cause. At first, it was more laughed at than reprimanded. However, it was beginning to get serious.

The teacher thought to herself, "Where is Jessica?" She scanned the room and spotted Jessica, who knew she was in trouble.

The cute act should get her out of trouble, as it had worked in the past, bopping up to the teacher with the cutest little pig tails ever. She flaunted and batted her big blue eyes, which were as big as dinner plates. The teacher, unfazed by the act, caused the child to change. Jessica now cowered like a poor broken animal that got caught doing something wrong.

The teacher began a police style investigation, full of over the top raves and rants. "Why on earth would you do such a gross thing? I'm serious, this is disgusting. What on earth could you possibly be thinking? What are you thinking? I am calling your parents!" While this went on the teacher's aide contacted Jessica's parents.

Jessica responded in a childlike fashion. "I don't know." After 30 or more of the over dramatic "I don't knows," the teacher was done. She instructed the aide to help Jessica gather up her things and escort her out. This was the last straw. Jessica would be expelled.

In the hallway, Jessica waited with the aide for her parents. Jessica licked the aide. The parents had just arrived and saw the aide being licked. They quickly scooped up their child and did not even bother to apologize before leaving the school.

After the embarrassment at the school and having the incident highlighted in the news, Jessica's parents believed they needed to reestablish themselves in a new community. They picked a quaint small town far away and believed they had "licked" their problem.

Chapter 11
The Recluse

Well overgrown and neglected for several decades, the dilapidated cemetery sat on a five-acre lot. Gravestone inscriptions were unrecognizable. Many lay crumbled and half-buried in the ground. The town's patriarch and a famous author were buried there. If you could get close enough to the patriarch's gravestone it read:

OUR BELOVED FOUNDER

ERICK HOFFMAN

HE LIVED **L**IFE TO THE

FULLEST

However, only four letters were legible;

HELL

While thankfully not coming from the cemetery, the moans and groans were mounting. The dilapidated cemetery was a nagging subject regularly brought up during town hall meetings. Jane, who was the mayor, could no longer stomach this constant burden.

As mayor of a relatively small town, (population 1,000), she knew removing the eyesore could no longer be put off. The town had little money in the coffers and any hint of a tax increase would probably get her lynched. Maybe not lynched, but it would definitely slay any hopes for reelection. She needed an idea that was fresh, cool. An unexpected epiphany came to the mayor while she vacationed with her family.

Family fun ahead equated to only 600 miles both ways in the family minivan. This was going to be a long trip and it had not even begun. Thankfully, the minivan's DVD player always served as the great equalizer for the rambunctious "Are we there yet?" children. Looping on the DVD player was her kids' favorite show, The Zombie Awesome Posse.

By default, the parents had become super fans. It was their extremely guilty pleasure. They coveted the times when the children watched the show. When their kids were distracted by who knows what and proceeded to leave the room, the parents "accidently" forgot to change the channel.

They knew their kids could never find out that they loved the show. When you like something your kids like, an automatic signal is sent to the child's brain telling them this is not good anymore. The child then develops a complete and utter disdain for something they loved just five seconds ago.

Halfway through the trip the mayor realized that the Zombie Awesome Posse was a perfect theme for a community event.

The Zombie Awesome Posse Festival was soon to be the most viewed on the internet, but not in a good way.

Big donations and dollar signs were in the mayor's eyes. To achieve a shindig of the imagined magnitude, the neighboring big city would need to be involved. This equated to the largest festival ever held in this small town.

Small, the town was always to remain small. The town's power players had made this an unofficial law. They loathed the previous mayor who went rogue on the town's core values. The previous mayor, not going through the proper formal channels, had wanted to fix the cemetery with a loan from one of the big city banks. A special election was held when the loan was sniffed out. The previous mayor stepped down even before the special election was held, knowing that winning was an impossibility.

The town's unwillingness for anything big, made the mayor's plans difficult. If the mayor tried to get together or even speak with the town's power players, it would be shut down. The mayor was going to have to pull out the "daddy card." Her daddy absolutely loved his only child. He called her "pudding pop" and in his eyes, she could do no wrong.

Her father ran the local barbershop. The barbershop was very similar to the Mafia controlled Italian restaurant. There were hardly any cars in the parking lot and no one was ever seen going in for a haircut. If you wanted something done, this is where you really began.

The mayor's oldest child's birthday was going to be a big hoopla and where the mayor would hit up her father. The mayor headed over to her father's work, batted her eyes and started with the long drawn-out childish annunciation, "Daddy." Her father knew she wanted something. Pudding Pop asked and Pudding Pop was going to get her festival. Her father personally saw to it.

The entire town would soon be taken over by a wide variety of characters from The Zombie Awesome Posse. The mayor would play the villain, Victoria Voodoo. The mayor ensured flyers, phone calls, and emails announced this event.

One flyer with a picture of an Uncle Sam zombie read:

The zombie outbreak is upon us. Become a hero and defend your town.

The Zombie Awesome Posse wants YOU!!!

Extra care had been taken and several phone calls were made the day before and the day of the event. The police proactively updated and placed an additional automated 911 message. The message was also available in Spanish.

"For zombie or the living dead rising incidents please press 1. For all other emergencies please press 2."

Callers who pressed 1 received this automated message.

"The community is putting on an event involving a mock zombie or living dead event. If your life is in imminent threat or you have another emergency please press 2."

Jack looked out his window in sheer terror. He was a shut-in and hadn't left his home in years. Sheltered for much of his life, he had little interaction with people and had no flavor for the current technology of TV, phones, or even the internet. Most of his days were spent reading and whittling wooden animals. The detail was explicit and these animals where periodically sold, as his only source of income. His family would help sell the items, in exchange provided his basic necessities. Business was so good, he was forced to renovate. He was beginning to add an extension to his home and a tarp replaced the once sturdy brick wall.

He knew Halloween was around the corner, so for a third time he reviewed his calendar. It was clearly September. He even drew enough courage to pick up the phone and call his family to verify. He asked for the date and then hung up. His family was concerned, but not concerned enough to follow up.

He had no gun, but knew he had to act swiftly. He had a naval officer sword, inherited from his father, who had fought in the First World War. He loved this sword, often fancying himself wielding it like a Samurai warrior. This passion grew into an obsession and he believed himself to be quite proficient in the art of Samurai. Actually, he was more proficient in the readings of the Samurai. He had only picked up the sword a handful of times. Jack wielded the sword. Nervously he readied himself for action.

Voodoo Victoria was on the run. Her powers were drained after an exhausting fight. The Zombie Awesome Posse and the entire town had her on the ropes. She saw Jack's house as a possible place to hide and allow her powers to regenerate. This was scripted to be part of the grand finale. Voodoo Victoria rushed inside and took cover under the tarp.

Jack's heart raced as he watched the hideous monster take refuge in his house. He said, "This will not do," and engaged the monster. He swung and effectively ended the life of the precious wooden eagle he had so diligently carved out years ago. Voodoo Victoria was terrified. He swung again and scored a hit. He heard a loud scream and saw red. Slowly he approached and was about to issue the death blow.

A large swarm of zombies converged on Jack's house as they heard screams. Jane opened her eyes and found The Zombie Awesome Posse. She had lost consciousness during the attack and her arm lay beside her, completely severed off. Before she regained consciousness, one of the zombies, who practiced medicine, was able to stop the bleeding. She doesn't remember screaming or really what happened all together. The one thing she should be thankful for was the fact that the art of the Samurai books Jack read did not teach him how to actually use the sword.

As Jack went for the potential death blow, the handle slipped out of his sweaty hands and flew through the air. Jack, already panic stricken, and blind with rage, desperately reached for the sword. He tripped and fell. Finally, he found his sword. In all the chaos he had not grabbed the sword this time. Jack began violently swinging a hair brush. The hair brush was an antique and weighed about the same as the sword. After this incident, people would joke that Jane did not see this "combing." Jack immediately turned his attention to the swarming zombie hoard. Still armed with the hairbrush, he lurched and struck a small zombie. Not standing for this, he was tackled and secured.

Jack would later say he was never informed about the event and believed Jane to be a real monster. A flyer was placed in his mail box, which he unknowingly threw away. He had hung up a half dozen times on the phone notifications. His family had been told of the event, but simply assumed he knew. He would also say that in his horrified state there was no time to call 911.

Jack's life was not the same since the incident. He was constantly heckled by most of the community. Teenagers tormented him relentlessly, they dressed up as zombies who would then run up to the door and shout, "I'm combing to get you." This past Halloween, fake limbs were attached to hairbrushes and strung across the huge maple tree in front of his house.

He quickly and quietly moved out. He could not be any happier with the new house and its community. They welcomed him, having no idea about his past incident. The mandatory counseling and a steady stream of medications would help further his overall happiness.

So how could this be happening again?

Chapter 12
Stranger's
Investment

For centuries, the King had constantly pondered his cursed life. He never knew that bees were the cause of his demise. They would again be part of a certain god's continued cruel plans.

He now resembled a wandering hobo-like creature. His cursed state allowed for no peace of mind or even sleep. Any semblance of rest could only be found in the act of blinking. He wandered endlessly with a lone companion of unappeasable hunger.

A new sensation of fatigue drew him to find a resting place. The cave was not a place for royalty, but it would do. He laid down on the cold damp dirt floor and was soon fast asleep. Not at all a blissful slumber, but one filled with his nightmarish past.

He dreamed of his army being annihilated by its villagers. The most awful screams and images haunted him as women and children tore through his once unstoppable army.

Oh those screams!

Those horrible screams!

He loved his army almost as much as he had once loved himself. If he could shake those cries, his finally experienced sleep would have been tolerable. However, he woke to those same screams.

He had avoided all human contact, which lessened his torturous thoughts, but not his desire for human flesh. If the King even got the slightest scent of a human, the need to feed would overtake him. Upon awakening, a sense of mission overtook him. This put aside his hunger.

A pilgrimage began towards a well populated area. The direction was dictated by the sound of buzzing bees. A long arduous hike led to a small bee farm. A bee keeper wondered why the bees were acting in such an agitated state.

A stranger was seen off in the distance heading towards the bee farm. This must be why the bees were distraught.

Now the stranger stood at the farm's entrance. Curiously, one of the bee keepers goes to greet the stranger. Before the stranger was reached the bee keeper could smell someone badly in need of some deodorant. After a brief conversation the bee keeper was off to fetch the owner. The stranger patiently waited.

The message relayed to the owner, drew him out. Cautiously he approached the stranger who wanted to buy his bee farm. The owner had thought of one day selling, but never took any efforts to even find appropriate suitors.

Would he sell? Only if the price was right. He was of retirement age and had grown weary of the angst of operating his own business.

It took the owner longer to reach the stranger than to complete the actual business transaction. Before any words were exchanged a rather large bag of gold coins was presented. The owner's eyes grew wide as the bag opened. He peeked in and immediately was taken aback. The owner considered himself quite an aficionado of coins. In all his days of collecting, he had never seen ancient coins of such high quality. Coin photos in books didn't even appear this perfect. The deal was struck. Gleefully and nervously the owner took the bag.

The stranger was the proud new owner of the bee farm.

Chapter 13
You Are
What You Eat

The new owner could not be pleased with his new investment. Shrinking profit margins combined with a past issue made for a shaky start. This all began when the new owner took over.

Several years ago, the bee farm, experienced a situation of much bewilderment. Bees, for some reason, vanished. What occurred in that case appeared to be a reproduction issue.

Expecting the same results, the beehives were examined. A most astonishing find was revealed. Reproduction was fine. In fact it, was accomplished at a phenomenal rate. What they did find was bee cannibalism. The queens devoured their own bees.

Removed, poked, and prodded was how the queens would spend the rest of their days. Rigorous tests, mainly genetic and physical, were conducted. No answers ever came from the tests.

New queens were purchased. Several precautions were taken before the queens were brought to the farm. Although no findings came from the testing, the new queens were subjected to the same tests as the old queens. These new queens received a clean bill of health and old hives were destroyed.

This incident sparked a unique idea to artificially manufacture honey. Research and Development began on this highly challenging and complex process, labeled HONEYPOT. Systematically, they were able to artificially produce bees wax and honey.

The process to produce both the honey and bees wax involved a BEECUBATOR (patent pending). Nectar was taken from flowers using the BEECUBATOR's long thin microscopic tubes. While passing through the tubes, the nectar was chewed for about an hour. The chewing process was basically the churning of the honey. A variety of proteins and vitamins were added during this phase. After chewing the nectar, it was either spread into honeycombs where the water was evaporated and allowed to cool or sent for conversion into wax. This was the artificial process of honey and wax making. The process could be manipulated to change, replace or remove the actual honey taste.

Some workers questioned why tinker, even remove the honey taste. The owner responded with a question of his own. He asked them if they thought everyone liked the taste of honey. At the same time they all responded with a resounding no. The owner then stated that the company's customer base would be expanded exponentially, if product lines included a variety of flavors.

Competing bee farms began to disappear. They had not experienced the bee cannibalism. No, they experienced a much deadlier "ISM." That is capitalism. The new artificial production process allowed for the severe undercutting of prices.

The company branched out and ventured into new markets. Each of the markets entered grew to monopolistic proportions. A sample of their diverse portfolio included technology, medicines, food, and entertainment.

Chapter 14
Vitamins & Cereals

A children's vitamin and cereal line was launched. The vitamin line was available in a variety of tablet forms (chewable, soluble, modified release, and sugar coated) entered the world market first. A well-known food and drug agency hailed this as the smart solution for the brain.

The vitamin came in all the shapes of The Zombie Awesome Posse characters. Boys loved the zombie male heroes. When squeezed, the vitamin would ooze a long sticky blood red line from the head. After downing the ooze, the body of the zombie was consumed. Equally beloved was the vitamin where a candy coated brain would pop out. Everywhere, little kids could be heard saying "brains."

Girls adored the pretty princess zombie shapes. Unlike the disgusting aspects of the boys vitamin, girls could mix and match accessories of their favorite characters. The accessories were sold separately from the characters. The most valued accessory was the limited edition stilettos, which upon their release, sold out within hours. They were available at various online auction sites, and sold for several hundreds of dollars.

The vitamin success spawned "The Zombie Awesome Posse O's cereal." As part of a healthy breakfast, the cereal consisted of a crispy skin-like outside with a soft red marshmallow inside. As with any cereal, the prize was more coveted than the cereal itself.

The front of the cereal box cover read, "A once in a lifetime prize. Could you be the newest villain of The Zombie Awesome Posse?" Entrants were required to send a photo of themselves along with an original character name. Odds of winning were 1 in 1,000,000.

The winner and newest villain was Victoria Voodoo. She was a voodoo zombie, bent on the destruction of The Zombie Awesome Posse. She envied and was overly jealous of the popular brain hungry zombie.

Chapter 15
Poor State

The state that Zack resided in was in deep financial trouble. Ballooned pensions and the loss of a major manufacturing plant brought the state one step closer to bankruptcy. An option presented itself that was too tempting for the cash strapped state to pass up.

The deal tied the state to a laundry list of requirements. Even the most paranoid zombie conspiracy theorist would never believe this was happening:

Clinical testing was needed for all ages and ranked in order of need:

1. Recently deceased – Any dead longer than a week will not be accepted.
2. Organ donations – The fresher the better.
3. Live participants.

Difficult, if not impossible to find, was the spelled out benefits for the state. Especially since the deal was done with a wink and a nod. No emails were sent, phone conversations were done on prepaid phones, and the money paid was laundered squeaky clean.

A hint of corruption came from the Governor's Office. The Governor began annual trips to Hawaii. The trips were to one of the plushest Hawaiian timeshares.

The leftovers were still enough to bail the state out of its pension problems. The state even reduced the tax rate for businesses in order to encourage economic growth. A company whose business was honey took advantage of the tax break and built a brand new facility in the state. It was well secured and hidden in a very rural part of the state. Zack would be the first nonemployee to visit the new facility.

Zack was in trouble with the law again. No matter how hard he tried he could not get his act together. Why can't he catch a break? He just needed another chance. After all, it was never his fault. Those around him knew better. He was never going to pull it together.

Strike four awaited him. He was going away for life. Strike three was thrown out due to a clerical error which listed him as a first-time offender.

A sensible person would ask the following before starting any clinical trial:

1. What is the compensation?

Compensation will be based on the level of participation. There are several different types of clinical trials each ranging in patient intrusion. The more required of the participant the higher the compensation. The participant can earn as much as $15 per hour.

2. What is the testing for?

Testing will be generic in nature. A one-on-one interview, combined with a standard test, will dictate what you will be tested for. A new vitamin is being tested for unknown and unwanted side effects.

3. What will I be subject to, anything painful?

Your pain threshold will dictate what you are subject to and your compensation. During the trial, your treatment and progress will be monitored more closely than if you were receiving general medical care.

4. Are there any side effects?

As with any treatment, you cannot be sure of the outcome. It is possible that you will experience unexpected side effects.

Below are the listed side effects from the test:

1. Restlessness
2. Sleep walking
3. Limited motor skills
4. Headaches
5. Paranoia
6. Sleepiness
7. Impaired speech
8. Stiffness
9. Cold sweats
10. Sense of indestructibility

NOTE: The list of side effects was ever increasing, as the number of products tested and number of people tested grew. However, this was the only list that ever saw the light of day.

5. Will this affect me physically and emotionally?

You may experience effects that are positive or negative. Please report them if you experience either.

6. What if I experience any problems after the trial ends and whom do I contact?

After the trial(s) have been finished, health professionals will be better able to offer you the most appropriate and effective treatment. Please contact the number provided upon departure from the clinic.

7. Will someone be available 24 hours a day?

There is an established 24 hour help line. Please call the help line prior to contacting anyone else, especially 911. We are the best equipped to treat whatever troubles you.

But how can one be reasonable when faced with life in jail? A lifeline was given as the judge offered him 15 years in a certain new facility. He thought that this was way too good to be true. He actually leapt for joy in the court room when the judge handed down his sentence.

Once hardnosed, the judge found clever ways to double the harshest sentences. Now almost all verdicts were the same. As the judge's financial problems landed him in the hip pocket of corruption.

A major portion of his retirement was lost in a ponzi scheme. He would end up investing heavily in the scheme he knew full well there would be no monetary gain. The reason was his beloved son had scammed unsuspecting victims out of millions.

The judge knew the exact figure $2.3 million. He had the money and power to make the issue go away. Those who had been scammed agreed not to bring a lawsuit if they received their money back with a little interest. While this did not financially break the judge, his own personal vanity would.

Chapter 16
Vanity

At an early age, the newly elected judge experienced what he considered a sneak peek into an early mid-life crisis. What else can be expected when you begin to lose the love of your life? Every day it was the same agonizing exploration of options. The judge thought that there had to be a cure for something so common. No one else in his family had this issue. Why him?

His loving wife, son, and co-workers supported him unconditionally. They did however secretly laugh and make fun of him behind his back. His frequently depressed mood led him to isolation and even fits of rage. The judge would often take refuge in others that experienced his similar problem.

No longer able to stand this shadow of a man she once knew and loved, his wife divorced him. He felt the divorce, while costly, was a gift, as he had emotionally separated himself long ago from his wife. Vanity led him to this self prescribed massive dose of great misfortune, the profit he experienced from his toils would only be deep sorrow and grief.

The judge was going bald. Not just a little, but a lot. The horseshoe outline that sat on top of his head was insufferable to the judge, especially someone who absolutely was in love with his prior thick wavy locks. Each morning his pillow, hair brushes, and shower drain were examined for any signs of hair. He had tried all the supposed solutions; hair plugs, all the name and non-name brand hair elixirs, and even hair that could come from a can. Nothing worked.

While presiding over a case, the judge found a solution. An employee was being brought up on charges by a company that had developed a wonder drug. In documents submitted to the court, the judge read what the drug could help with:

1. Depression
2. Strength inhibitor
3. Aging

4. Baldness

5. Hunger

Number four definitely caught his attention. Noting the cure for baldness, the judge did something he never believed himself cable of doing. During the hearing, a motion to dismiss the case was asked by the defense, citing a lack of evidence. It was hard to believe as the person was not only caught on video, but was also caught selling the wonder drug to an undercover police officer. A break in the chain of custody led the evidence to never see the light of day and it magically disappeared. The judge agreed the motion was justified and dismissed the case. During the dismissal the judge verbally attacked the prosecutor that had forced the judge's hand, "I am sick and tired of having to issue these rulings for what should be open and shut cases. These failures on the part of the state are appalling. Today is another black eye for the justice system. I hope you can live with yourself."

After the trial the employee's union forced the company to rehire the employee with back pay. The employee would soon receive a visit from the judge. They made an arrangement, at a premium price, for the judge to get the drug.

A costly divorce, paying his kid's way out of trouble and an expensive vanity habit made the judge easily susceptible to corruption. Eventually the judge had issues paying for his addiction. This began the judge's slippery slope into corruption.

The judge would become the source to provide live participants for the clinical trials.

Chapter 17
Belly Flop

Zack, who thought he was a rock star, began his sentence at the facility. He loved to be the center of attention and was more than happy to weave his favorite tale to any listeners. Born on a belly flop, Zack would often joke.

You see Zack came from a long line of circus folk. His mother was circus; her mother was circus and so on. The circus family's claim to fame was a unique performance.

Now announcing the one, the only:

THE TRIPLE SYNCHRONIZED
CANNON DIVE

Intro:

Looky, loaded, ready to be launched.

Song:

Before you go inside
You are welcome to close your eyes
But leave open your mind
So you can picture this
Three lovely ladies flying through the
sky

No strings
No wings
Nor any of those silly things

This explains the reason why

Man was not meant to fly

These lovely ladies will be blasting

by

High enough to touch the sky

While they're there

A cloud will experience a tear

Before the tear can fritter away

The ladies will have found their way

So grasp your seats

The following cannot be beat

It is after all today's most spectacu-

lar treat

The dive was unlike any other. Three individuals simultaneously were shot out of a cannon. They soared like eagles over their crowds and achieved heights where the clouds could be pierced. A variety of flips and tricks but mostly spins of over 720 degrees were performed. They finally landed gracefully into individualized small pools of water.

Three thinly shaped women were part of his mother's cannon dive trio. Her figure only showed the slightest hint of being an expectant mother. His mother never told anyone she was pregnant, not even his father. She would continue her family's cannon dive tradition regardless of any risk. This is how circus folk are.

During one performance there was a minor hiccup. While flying through the air, the crowd experienced an unexpected, short downpour. The stunned crowd's eyes were momentarily taken away from the performers, now directed towards the sky where no clouds appeared. The mother's water had broken.

For some reason this distracted the expectant mother. Her landing was a big ole belly flop. This shot a baby out.

Half the crowd cheered; the other half threw up. Was this part of the act? The answer of course is the birthing of Zack.

Whether Zack's story was true or not was unknown. It does speak to his character, as his imagination was constantly in overdrive. He fancied himself to be a future acclaimed author. Like many self-proclaimed authors before him, he only conjured up a few pages.

Chapter 18
Zombie Sex

Humans need to stop unjustly profiling. Placing zombies in a box is discrimination. Zombies are more than the overly portrayed mindless, soulless flesh eaters. Aside from bringing down humanity, zombies do pursue other endeavors.

At one time human, zombies have kept most of their prior thoughts, desires, and needs. Just like humans, zombies crave sex. Zombies have all the appropriate body parts, so why not? Also, zombies must preserve their own race.

Zombies, however, are not sexual deviants like humans. The average male zombie only thinks about sex every ten minutes, as opposed to male humans five minutes. Female zombies and female humans find all males equally annoying.

This brings up an important question. Are zombie attacks and the horizontal tango that similar? Examining and distinguishing between the two may actually help understand the fascination with zombies. The chart below shows how closely a zombie attack is to sex (check the box for sex or zombie attack):

	SEX	ZOMBIE ATTACK
Looks better on TV.		
It could happen at any time or place.		
A big hoopla equates to a few minutes.		
It's not the length or the size. It's the number of times.		
Individuals may or may not know each other.		
Rejection may only serve as encouragement.		
If rejected, another selection is made.		
Multiple positions, missionary is the norm.		
Savoring your victims, I mean partners smells and taste.		
A fair amount of moaning, groaning, convulsing, and some biting.		
Distorted faces.		
Inability to walk correctly.		
Upon completion you start thinking of the next time.		

Chapter 19
Zombie Good vs. Zombie Bad

The King was the beginning, the firstborn of the undead, that all things he himself might be preeminent. Rebirthing of the king laid the foundation for the apocalypse. If only he had stayed in the cave, never to have risen again. If only he had not purchased the bee farm.

The life of a zombie was never an option. The event, or better yet the defining moment, was when humanity unknowingly subjected themselves to a variety of products from a particular honey company. No one knew, not even the King, that his mere presence infected the vats of the artificially made honey.

The Bakers', a wrestler, a depressed young girl, a community organizer, a judge, and a career criminal make for a very unruly cast of characters. They are also my acquaintances in the hoard I find myself in. Aside from being bad zombies, we have little in common, except that we used products from the honey company.

Becoming a zombie is a chemical reaction. The amount and frequency of the addictive chemical ingested determines how fast the conversion takes place. This, however, does not define a zombie as good or bad. The key is whether a person has an appendix or not.

The overly documented useless organ is no longer that useless after all. Through evolution the human appendix has lost any real functionality. It has been speculated that the appendix is a redundant organ serving as a safe house for good bacteria. The good bacterium in the appendix turns out to be the critical factor in determining a zombie being good or bad.

Now the good zombie is not going to be escorting elderly ladies across streets. No, the good zombie isn't earning that badge. A good zombie gets no satisfaction, nor do they have the ability to digest zombie flesh. Great pain is experienced if zombie flesh is eaten.

Good zombies cannot even stand to be around other zombies, good or bad. This is why a lone zombie is often seen wandering in no particular direction at all. Only when it is time to hunt humans do good zombies even team up.

"Appendix Gratis" (appendix free) is the bad zombie. A bad zombie eats humans and zombies alike. However, humans are preferred, as the gratification from consumed zombie flesh is not even a close second.

So come get your flesh fixings with the prime rib of humanities terror. The zombie apocalypse is upon you. However it is not all bad, well at least not for zombies.

Chapter 20
Zombie
Apocalypse in 3D

"Hurry up, hurry!"

"They're coming!"

"There's no time!"

"Just take what you can!"

They were being overwhelmed. There was real trouble and backup was required. The moans were becoming unbearable. Alex was needed up front as soon as possible.

Just in time, Alex brought up reinforcements and saved the day. They had run out of guns and the 3D printer used to print additional guns was jamming again. The guns were the hit of the Expo and after several hours the line quieted down.

He had worked feverishly and was completely exhausted. Alex, took a moment, and breathed a satisfying sigh of relief. He finally found his chance for a break.

In the concession area he ate his fat free, gluten-free free cream cheese bagel, when the sound of moaning returned. Why was there moaning? Staring out of the glass building, Alex saw what appeared to be a hoard of zombies. At first he laughed. Then he saw several of those zombies bringing down and tearing into some helpless victim. Blood splattered on the glass, which woke Alex from a state of disbelief. The building erupted into chaos.

The building's security had set up a short-term reinforcement of the doors before the zombies could penetrate the entrance. Those who had not helped to secure the building hid or were helping set up a defense.

The reinforced doors did not hold up. Zombies entered by the hundreds and are immediately fired upon. In a sick twisted way, it was funny to see that for each zombie taken down, the weapon used shattered. 3D guns are not known for lasting, they broke after only a few shots. Those guns are now paperweights at best, as they were thrown or used like a hammer to bash the zombies.

The defenses built seemed more like the Alamo, as they were eventually breached and left no survivors. However, a piece of Alex did escape. A zombie, who was on a gluten-free diet, spitted out Alex's tongue. It reeked of Alex's meal. The Expo, Alex, and his meal had become the first chapter in the zombie apocalypse.

After the Expo massacre the zombies' exploits only increased in intensity and inventiveness. A month passed by and the world population was cut in half. Another quarter of the population was slashed, thanks to humans being so darn gullible.

Chapter 21
Zombie Tales

The slow, moaning, and crooked zombie approached. Three bullets whizzed by, not even coming close. Thankfully, the zombie approached at tortoise speed. The six-chambered gun took time to load, especially since the operator appeared to have never handled a gun before.

The shooter rifled through his pants pocket, a handful of bullets were dug out. All but six bullets were returned. The gun was slowly reloaded with four bullets. This should have been enough to take down a lone attacker.

Greedily, the person thought that it would be a good idea to load the empty chambers. The shooter thought, "You never know if another zombie could be around the corner." A sound strategy, if the last two bullets had not fallen to the ground.

Momentarily his concentration was taken away from the zombie, as he reached for the two bullets beside his foot. A smile appeared on the zombie's face. It was time for lunch. A full sprint launched the overzealous zombie towards his distracted meal.

This strategy proved overly effective and was consistently used. The moaning combined with the stumbling zigzag slow walk served as a distraction to size up the intended prey. A head shot was the only way to bring down a zombie. As illustrated by the zombie's latest victim, most shooters could not hit the broad side of a battleship, especially given their panic-stricken and agitated state.

Zombie eat Zombie

Giggling like little school girls, a most dastardly plan was hatched.

It had been days since the last feast. Hunger gripped the hoard and it could no longer be contained. Suddenly, the hunt was on. The slippery slope of turning on each other had been breached.

Chad, a rather svelte zombie found the hoard chasing him. No one liked Chad, not even in his zombie life. This took disdain to a new and interesting level. Surprisingly, the hunt was over before it even began. Chad engorged himself on their catch. What happened?

This was no hunt, it was entrapment. George found himself to be an unknowing victim. He displayed a very noticeable limp, as he recently twisted his ankle. He was an ideal target.

This has been coined "zombie on zombie violence", likened to car driver's rear end insurance scam. It all starts with a chase. A single zombie maneuvers himself to be positioned slightly ahead of the unknowing victim. When in position, the zombie suddenly stops, forcing the victim down. Obviously shocked, the victim has little or no time to react as the group is already upon them. In one instance the zombie initiating the scam stumbled and found the roles reversed. Poor George was one of its casualties.

A zombie must be aware at all times of another zombie's modus operandi. Unlike the rear end scam, there is no insurance or law to help the victim. Zombie laws are only the law of survival.

Zombies need water

All forms of life require some form of hydration. Why would the Zombie be any different? Flesh does quench both hunger and thirst. As humans become scarce, this has caused large gaps between feedings. Zombies have begun exploring other forms of nourishment.

A zombie working party busily fills trucks with the basic zombie necessities. Water, sodas, coffee, alcohol, and liquor are the prime targets of this run. The order should begin with alcohol and liquor, as zombies love their booze.

Most zombies know that zombies can get drunk. However, this is not readily known to those new to their zombie forms. It was also not passed into their orientation to their new-found friends. What new zombies are told is that zombies can drink anything with no side effects.

A young couple just joined the group. They did not stand a chance. Especially since as they so boastfully told us during our latest grocery run that they loved a good bottle of wine.

POP!!!

The wine was uncorked. It was a very nice bottle with an excellent bouquet. Crystal wine glasses saw a generous portion of wine fill to the glasses brim. Glasses rise, toasting the day's hard work. The group sipped, while the young couple consistently knocked off one glass after another. Their heads bobbed even more than a typical zombie head. Looking into their eyes, one can tell they have achieved a buzz.

They ask why they felt this way. This was easily explained away as only a temporary side effect. The young couple wasn't even listening, having already poured another round. Eventually they literally drank their way into oblivion.

The group loved the opportunity the passed out young couple had provided them. Dinner and drinks all in one.

Zombie Diet

Does a bear poop in the woods? If it does, then a zombie would be its best friend.

A zombie's diet is heavy on protein, light on fiber and carbohydrates. Negative side effects of a protein rich diet includes bloating, constipation, and of course flatulence. The later in the list is more prevalent as a zombie's digestion rate is twice as fast as that of humans. This makes for a very stinky situation and introduces a strange new zombie practice.

Remnants of the last attack had been picked clean. The usual low moan of a zombie was soon replaced by a much more aggravated tone. Zombies must now deal with that nagging issue of getting rid of that darn crap out from between their teeth. Tongues would thrust and rub between teeth. Fingers plunged into mouths as nails poked at the issue. One zombie even tried using a sheet of paper, which annoyed his zombie significant other.

As an arborist by trade, Bob knew trees. He was also more than happy to share and lecture anyone within earshot. His next audience would be his zombie counterparts.

Bob pushed up his glasses with his index finger. Cracking a half smile, he whispered to himself, "Self, it's show time!"

He walked over to a small grassy area and shouted "Mentha piperita." This had drawn the attention of the zombie hoard. They gathered before Bob and he explained his bellow.

"Mentha piperita is peppermint. I have gathered everyone in this spot to be near peppermint plants. Use these to pick your teeth clean and then eat them. The best part is that the digestion of peppermint will help provide the relief for our multitude of hygiene issues. In layman's terms, relieve our zombie flatulence. As we all know, zombies fear zombie gas. Especially Jimmy's gas. Bob proceeded on and on about the history of peppermint, explaining that it was a hybrid and so on and so forth. Eyes rolled and the yawns began in the back of the audience.

One zombie in particular had a problem getting their eyes back in focus. In a vain attempt the poor zombie placed their hands over their eyes and shook their head excessively. Eye problems were a chronic problem for zombies. One zombie knew the cure and smacked the effected zombie in the head.

The audience would like to smack Bob in the head to get him to shut up. Instead of smacking, leaving or telling him to shut up they simply ate him and celebrated with some nice peppermint. "Thanks Bob," snickered the audience.

One positive factor of a zombie diet was that the absence of carbohydrates encourages weight loss. Many lady zombies brag about not being this size since their youth. A trip to the mall was definitely needed.

Chapter 22
The Exchange

From up on high Loki sat, ever so lovingly petting his mangled creation. The platypus purred satisfyingly with every loving pass. To say he was pleased understated Loki's current mindset. Watching the destruction of this much inferior race brought semisweet relief to an unquenchable desire for sadistic fun. He knew full well the demonstrative plans had just begun. But first he would relieve the cursed King, for a price.

The King's son's face narrowed as he thought, "Disgustingly fresh!" He knew what was expected and it would not be appetizing.

A single thick piece of flesh had been sliced off the conquered enemy's not yet dead body. Cut so precisely it could have come off a meat slicer. The raw bloody half pound of flesh dangled in front of the child, its consumption was awaited by all. A glorious roar was heard from the crowd as the child proudly and painfully ate the flesh of the victim. After ingested, the man child began to unsheathe his sword.

His armor was designed to be ultra durable, yet light-weight. It felt heavy after a long day's battle. It needed to be removed before the death blow would be delivered. The enemy's head was forced upon a chopping block. A precise blow severed the head from the body. Fondly, the King approached his son. A manly grip and then shake of the hand were exchanged. This completed the coronation process and the celebrations could now begin.

On the outskirts of town, near the most beautiful pond, a lavished party commenced. The king's son was traditionally sent ahead of his father and the army so the tale of the battle can be told. As the story was told, villagers listened intently, however their attention waned. A faint, consistent buzzing noise broke their attention.

Poor acoustics took a back seat to the large swarm of bees now descending upon the villagers. They helplessly flailed their arms in a futile attempt to thwart the swarm. Escape from the bees was only found at the bottom of the pond and the rest were stung. The venom from the swarm quickly transformed those stung into zombies, who exhibited the most ferocious of appetites. The hunger was aimed at the King and his army.

The first to reach the King was his now zombie son. The King experienced a feeling he had never felt before, sheer sadness and regret for what he knew was his own doing. After the villagers attacked, the King's curse began and those previously infected were converted back to their human forms.

Centuries passed, nevertheless the King's son held lingering tortured feelings over the death of his father. Not a moment went by when he was not tormented by this event. Hoping for relief, the son began an infinite plea for a deal with the gods.

After several more centuries, Loki finally took "pity" on the King's son. This was to be no simple exchange as the son had pleaded for, but another insidious, torturous game strictly for Loki's entertainment. The deal began as the King's curse was lifted, eventually sending him into a death slumber. The son would soon be accompanied by two others and become an additionally horror for humanity. He would serve as a plague for zombies. In nine months they would come into the world. The three new terrors would no longer have their given names, but would now be called Benjamin, Andrew, and Molly Baker...

Here's a sneak peek at:

The next book in the **CHASING THE ZOMBIE** series.

Preface

18, 19, 20, no 21 hours. Every time the story was rehashed the amount of time increased. The actual time was much less, maybe 15 hours. Regardless, the end result was three of the most heavenly blessing. At least that's what two of the three parents believed.

Only one of the three knew that these heavenly blessings were in reality a curse. Jill and Max Baker definitely had no clue. How could they? There was no reason for them to know. The one that did know had been on pins and needles waiting for this event.

This was going to be a stellar, very entertaining century for the God Loki. He had already planted the seed for the zombie apocalypse and was now about to be a proud parent. For the past nine months he had gone back and forth on several names:

Boys Names (The names were taken from Loki's Father, Farbauti)

1. Farren
2. Farley
3. Farid
4. Loki Jr.

Girls Names (The names were taken from Loki's Mother, Laufey)

1. Laurent
2. Faris

The Bakers chose the names; Benjamin, Molly, and Andrew. These names did not impress Loki. He would give them what he deemed as their rightful names when part 2 of the apocalypse was to begin.

Chapter 1
Prepper's Son

A dense forest and large electric barbed wire fence engulfed an entire facility. From the highway one could barely make out what was there, if you blinked you would miss it. The remote ultra secure facility was located off of exit 51.

The exit sign had been vandalized with graffiti. "Alien Gas" had become an unwelcome problem for this poor sign. The Doomsday Prepper's son was at it again...